SURPRISE ISLAND

Weekly Reader Children's Book Club presents

Surprise Island

Barbara Willard

Illustrated by JANE PATON

MEREDITH PRESS / New York

Contents

1   *A Bag of Biscuits*   3

2   *Full Particulars*   13

3   *Preparations*   23

4   *Entirely Surrounded by Water*   35

5   *Mr. Tapsell and Miss Tapsell*   47

6   *A Hole in the Water*   63

7   *Keep Out. Strictly Private*   79

8   *A Letter from Fullowag*   89

9   *The Final Result*   99

SURPRISE ISLAND

WEEKLY READER
CHILDREN'S BOOK CLUB

1

A Bag of Biscuits

There was nothing Jill and her friend Limpet enjoyed more than looking after Brandy when Mrs. Remnant was away for a few days. Brandy was partly theirs, anyway. He was such an enormous dog that he was easily shared among several people. Ever since Mrs. Remnant's trailer had been settled conveniently in Little Paddock, Jill and Limpet had taken a hand in arranging Brandy's life. Or perhaps it might be truer to say that Brandy arranged theirs, making it very plain to them when he felt a walk would be a good idea and sitting beside them quite quietly but dribbling slightly whenever they were eating chocolate or ice cream or cookies.

"Remember, really dash home after school," Jill said to Limpet the day Mrs. Remnant went off to visit her nephew. "I'll go and buy some dog biscuits—Mrs. Remnant's given me the money—and you go and collect his meat. I'll meet you at the trailer."

Limpet just nodded. He went off to school, humming to himself. He was used to taking orders from Jill and was almost always very good-tempered about it.

Little Paddock, where the trailer was pitched, was between Jill's father's nursery garden and Limpet's father's field. It belonged a little to both of them, and both had been glad to let Mrs. Remnant settle there with Brandy when she lost her home and had nowhere to go.

The school day ended at last. Limpet rushed off home where his father, Mr. Jeffreys the butcher, had a large parcel of juicy scraps wrapped up and ready. Meanwhile, Jill was impatiently waiting her turn in the village shop, where the owner and a customer were gossiping.

"A seven-pound bag of dog biscuits, please," Jill managed to ask at last.

"Meet-n-weet or Fullowag?"

"Meet-n-weet, please."

Away went the shopkeeper and stayed away for ages.

"I'm afraid we've only got Fullowag."

"Fullowag, then," said Jill, hopping with impatience, as she felt the minutes slipping by and knew how Brandy would be longing for his food. She put down the right money, seized the big bag, and rushed off

with it banging her legs as she ran. She wanted to get to
the trailer before Limpet. She wanted to be the one
who opened the door and let Brandy come bounding
out. Jill always liked to be first.

In fact she and Limpet arrived at exactly the same
moment. He came dashing down the steep field behind
his home; she came tearing along the path from hers.
They scrambled over their gates in precisely the same
few seconds.

Brandy had heard them coming. He had been alone
since midday, when Jill's mother had given him a run.
He was up on Mrs. Remnant's bunk, his great paws on
the narrow window frame, his tongue lolling, his little
eyes shining, his teeth grinning. Faraway, inside the

trailer, at the end of his great white-and-brown body, his tail waved very gently.

Jill and Limpet both dived for the trailer steps. They struggled to get ahead of one another and pull open the door. Out came Brandy, leaping through the opening, knocking them both backward so that they rolled over on the grass together, where he kept them as long as he could, banging and thumping them and huffing with his own kind of laughter. There was such a tangle of arms and legs and fur that it seemed as though they would never get themselves sorted out again.

At last Brandy decided that the game had lasted long enough. He sat back on his haunches and watched as the other two gradually recovered themselves and staggered to their feet. Then he dashed twice around the paddock and came back to them, skidding to a stop on the grass. He barked, not his usual quiet, polite bark, but a loud rude bark that demanded food.

"Come on," said Jill, grabbing up the bag of biscuits. "Bring the meat. I hope the knife's sharp. We ought to ask your father to sharpen it."

"He says it's quite sharp enough. He says if it's sharper it'll go right through the board."

Jill was used to Limpet's father, who thought—often quite rightly—that he knew more than anybody else. She said nothing but went into the trailer. Limpet and Brandy followed.

It was a lovely trailer. When Mrs. Remnant, after all her troubles, found she had enough money to buy a new trailer to put in Little Paddock, she decided to have the best. It was beautifully planned, with every possible bit of space filled up with tidy cupboards and drawers. The stove was the neatest ever seen, shining and clean. And since this was the kind of trailer that did not have to move from place to place, there was a little heating stove with a chimney. As it was spring, Mrs. Remnant had stood a pot of flowers on it to brighten it up.

Yet in spite of all these things, and in spite of the new curtains and covers, it was still not quite as cozy as the old converted bus Mrs. Remnant and Brandy had lived in when Jill and Limpet first knew them. That had been crammed full of pictures and ornaments and photographs, which Mrs. Remnant had had to get rid of when she thought she would not be able to live in a trailer again. No doubt they had all been rather a nuisance to keep clean, but Mrs. Remnant was a person who seemed to need a bit of muddle and clutter around her. Jill often hoped she would soon fill the new trailer as she had filled the old. She had her parakeets back, which was a good start.

"Give them some fresh water," Jill commanded Limpet, as she sliced up the meat. "I suppose your father thinks we'll cut ourselves if he sharpens the knife. But I think it's easier to cut yourself with a blunt knife, be-

cause you have to press so hard." And she sawed away
at the meat while Brandy sat and dribbled with longing.

"My Dad says we needn't cut the meat up so small."

"Brandy *hates* great hunks. . . . Let the parakeets
out for a bit, Limpet."

"They might get away. Mrs. Remnant would have a
fit."

"We wouldn't let them get away, silly."

Limpet said no more. He went ahead with seed and
water, but he did not let the parakeets out to fly about
and perch, as they often did, on Brandy's head. Limpet
was wonderfully patient with Jill, who was often ex-
tremely bossy. He was much more practical than she
was, so they made good partners. But although she
bossed him, Jill knew that once Limpet had made up
his mind he would not change it; so she did not mention the birds again but went on busily preparing
Brandy's meal.

At last the meat was in the dish. Limpet heaved up
the big bag of biscuits and opened it, and began adding
them to the dish. He piled it up, for Brandy was big
and needed a lot.

By this time Brandy had dribbled so much that there
was a horrid little puddle between his huge front paws.
He sprang up as Jill opened the door and went outside,
and as she put his dish down on the clipped grass by
the steps, he hurled himself after her. His nose went

into the dish as though he would burrow a hole in it.
Bits of biscuit flew out to left and right as he thrust
about to find the meat, which he always ate first. Later
he would snuffle over the grass until he had recovered
every missing crumb.

"You've put the ticket in the dish," Jill said to Limpet, as a slip of paper came flying out with the biscuits.
The ticket was there so that you could send it back and
complain to the maker if anything was wrong with the
bag of biscuits.

"Not the ticket," Limpet said, picking it up.

"What is it, then?"

"It's a message."

"From Mrs. Remnant? But I thought it came out of
the bag—and it's a new one."

"It isn't from Mrs. Remnant." Limpet undid the folded paper and spread it out. "It's a sort of advertisement." He sat down on the steps; Jill sat beside him and they read the paper together.

"Endless Sunshine Can Be Yours," they read aloud. "An Island in the South Seas Awaits You. Send for Full Particulars of Our Simple Contest. Open to All."

"Goodness," said Jill, "the South Seas. That's thousands of miles away."

"How do you get there?"

"Airplane, of course."

"Whatever would you do with an island if you won it?"

"Live on it, silly. Like it says, in endless sunshine." Jill stared at the paper. There was a little picture of the island. It had a lot of palm trees. All around the edge of the drawing were things like coconuts and pineapples. "We could all go," she said slowly. "You and me and Mummy and Daddy—he could grow orchids and make a lot of money. You can grow orchids in those places—I know you can because he's got a book about it. . . . And Mrs. Remnant and Brandy—we couldn't leave them behind." She paused a moment, struck by an awkward thought. "Would your father want to come, too?"

"Mom wouldn't."

"Well, if we did the simple contest together, the island would have to be half yours—so we could pay you some money for it," Jill decided, "and then you could come by yourself for all your vacations."

Limpet looked at Jill to see if she believed what she was saying. He could see that she did. She had decided what was going to happen. Limpet had known Jill's plans to go wrong before now, but she was always so positive that he could not help feeling things would happen as she said they would.

By this time Brandy had finished everything in his dish and had explored for crumbs between every blade of grass. He was ready for a walk. He stood and stared at Jill and Limpet, waving his tail, looking from face to face without moving his head. He barked once, very quietly—as if clearing his throat to attract their attention.

"Come on," said Jill. "Better not keep him waiting. Let's go to Windle Wood."

Windle was about half a mile away, beyond the end of the village. The wood was part of land belonging to Windle Lodge. Mr. Tapsell lived there, with his sister Constance. You could walk in the woods, for the fence was broken down, though there were notices saying TRESPASSERS WILL BE PROSECUTED, and PRIVATE. NO ENTRY. In fact, although it was easy to get through the broken fence, nobody seemed to do so except Jill and Limpet, and they never spoke about it at home. They walked there quietly, careful to keep within the shelter of the trees, knowing that they ought not to be there

and feeling a slight, exciting spice of danger. For anybody knew that if Mr. Tapsell caught trespassers on his
ground, he had plenty to say about it. He and his sister
did not take much part in the life of the village, though
Miss Tapsell did her shopping there, and Mr. Tapsell
was a customer of Hyde's Nursery. Their retiring ways
and the forbidding notices around their property made
people speak of them unkindly. But the notices were so
very old that they must have been put up first by Mr.
and Miss Tapsell's father—a frightening old man, who
had lived to the enormous age of a hundred and one.

It was lovely that afternoon as Jill and Limpet and
Brandy went through the wood together. The sun was
hot and golden. The leaves of the high beech trees and
of the narrow birches had never seemed so sharply
green. It made Jill think how wonderful endless sunshine must be, even if it was far away in the South Seas.

Presently they came to the edge of the wood and
stopped as they always did at that point. They looked
down a long, gentle green slope to a lake, not very big,
lying absolutely quiet in the hollow. Round about it
there were more trees, and these hid the house, Windle
Lodge, where the Tapsells lived.

There was something about the lake which neither
Jill nor Limpet had quite taken in until today. In the
middle was a tiny island.

2

Full Particulars

"Ours would be bigger," said Jill.

"And with more trees," said Limpet. There was only one on the little island in the middle of Windle Lake.

"Palm trees—lots of them. I expect we should have to cut some down to make room for a house."

"And lots of greenhouses for orchids," Limpet reminded her.

"Oh, they'd grow in the garden, I think. . . . Where's the paper about it?"

Limpet pulled out the folded paper from his pocket and once more they read it through, this time more carefully.

"We must send for full particulars at once!" cried Jill. "Look at the date—it ends on the twentieth! Thank goodness Mrs. Remnant went away today—another week and we might never have known about it."

Their letter went off in the next morning's mail and Jill immediately began waiting for a reply.

"Perhaps we were too late," she said on the second morning. "Perhaps we didn't give the address properly. Perhaps the letter got lost in the mail. . . ."

"Sit down and get on with your breakfast," her mother said.

Her father looked up from the letter he was reading.

"What's all the fuss about, Jill?" And he went on to say to his wife, "Here's an order from old Tapsell, Margaret. Five dozen roses for next autumn. I hope I've got all he wants."

"The island, Daddy," Jill said. "You know. I told you."

"So you did. We're all going to the South Seas to grow coconuts—isn't that it?"

"Orchids!"

"You haven't told me how you're going to win this island." He looked across the table at his wife, and although he did not quite wink, Jill could hear the wink in his voice.

"I don't know yet," she said. "That's the trouble. The full particulars haven't arrived."

"They'll turn up. Do you have to send any money— do you have to pay to enter the contest?"

"No—you just send some labels off Fullowag bags."

"Fullowag bags the lot," he said, laughing at his own joke.

His wife said "Really, John!" But she laughed, too. Even Jill laughed a bit, and Brandy, who generally came to breakfast when Mrs. Remnant was away, slid out from his place under the table to discover what was happening.

Fortunately the letter Jill was waiting for arrived the next morning. She could not possibly open it without Limpet, for he had paid for half the stamps on the letter they had had to send for particulars. It was Saturday, so she dashed off to Little Paddock the instant breakfast was over. Limpet was already sitting on the gate, waiting for her.

"It's come! It's come!" she cried, waving the letter as she ran to join him, with Brandy bounding ahead.

They could hardly wait to tear the envelope open. Inside was a big folded sheet of paper. The rules of the contest were printed on one side, at the bottom there was a form that would have to be filled in, and on the other side were rows and rows of small pictures of dogs. They soon discovered that you had to write under each one what kind it was. There were fifty different dogs.

"It's easy!" cried Jill.

Limpet said nothing. He held the paper a long time, looking at the rows of different dogs.

" 'Tisn't so easy, Jilly. What's that one—look?"

"Some sort of spaniel, of course."

"But *what* sort?"

Jill did not reply, but took the paper and gazed at it in her turn. She could not help seeing what Limpet meant. Many of the dogs looked dreadfully alike. There was even one that looked like a Pekinese—until you saw that there was an obvious Pekinese in the next row.

"Get your dog book, Limpet."

"Now?"

"Yes."

He ran off at once. Jill watched him go. His father was just the sort of person who might be able to help with naming the fifty dogs. But if he helped he would have to share the island with them; otherwise it wouldn't be fair. That would be nice for Limpet, of course, but Jill felt it would be much less than nice for the rest of them.

She sat down on the steps of the trailer and looked again and again at the rows of dogs, big and little, curly and flat-coated, long-tailed, short-tailed and no-tailed.

"That's you, Brandy," she said, showing him the St. Bernard, number five in the top row. "Only you are much more beautiful."

Brandy sat and grinned and panted a bit in the hot, sunny morning. Then he gave one of his enormous sighs and leaned hard against Jill, as he did when he was feeling very loving. She put her free arm around him, then she dropped the paper and used both arms to hug him, he was so wonderful. In fact, as she sat there in the sunshine in Little Paddock, Jill did just wonder for a second why anyone should want to leave home and go to live on an island in the South Seas. . . .

Limpet was back in no time with his dog book, a piece of paper and two pencils—he was always very businesslike.

"My Dad says write on the paper first—make a list. Then if we go a bit wrong it won't matter."

Mr. Jeffreys was certainly the most sensible man in the world. How dreadful it would have been if they had spoiled the entry form and had no time to send for another.

"We can't take long over this, you know," Jill said. "It's got to get there by next Wednesday. . . . Goodness—that means we must mail it on Monday or it might not get there. We've only got today and to-morrow!"

Limpet had picked up the paper that Jill had thrown down when she made a fuss over Brandy. He was looking at it carefully, frowning as he did so.

"There's something else here," he said.

"What else? What do you mean?"

" 'Tisn't only the dogs' names. . . ."

"*What* isn't only the dogs' names? Oh, do talk sense," cried Jill, very worked up because he looked so solemn. "Give me the paper—I want to see."

Limpet hung on. "It's on the back. When we've done the dogs we've got to make up a—" He broke off and spelled it out under his breath "—s-l-o-g-a-n. A sloggan."

"What does it *mean?* Read it aloud!"

"A sloggan in not more than ten words giving your dog's opinion of Fullowag."

There was a brief, sharp silence of dismay, then Jill broke out in a rage. "But that's not fair. It said 'a simple contest. . . . Send for full particulars of our simple contest,' it said. It just isn't simple. . . . And it isn't sloggan, it's slogan."

"Sloggan is a better word," said Limpet. "Here—take your pencil and paper. See how many you can write down."

He sat on the top step of the trailer. He seemed very busy and sure of himself. He appeared to know the sort

of thing to write, while Jill was completely at a loss—
she just could not get down one single word. She just
sat chewing her pencil and feeling frantic.

"If only Brandy could tell us what he thinks of Fullowag. It would be easy then."

"It wouldn't be fair," said Limpet, sternly. "Don't
chatter please. I'm thinking."

Jill nearly pushed him off the step in her annoyance.

He was scribbling away as though he had been doing
just this kind of work all his life.

"I've got six," he said at last. "How many have you
got?"

"Tell me yours," said Jill, cautiously.

"Is this any good? A full bag of Fullowag fills me full
of wags."

"That's more than ten words—it must be."

"It's exactly ten."

"What are the others, then?" He was being very clever indeed, and she knew she ought to say so. She hated to admit how exceedingly unclever she was being herself.

"Time for supper, time for Fullowag. Or—Nothing wags like bags of Fullowag. And—Bags I my bag of Fullowag. Or—Wot, no Fullowag? Or—"

"The first is the best," said Jill. "Let's send that." And she quickly crumpled her paper because she could not bear his knowing that she had thought of absolutely nothing.

"A full bag of Fullowag fills me full of wags." Limpet repeated it two or three times. "I don't think it's quite right. You say it, Jilly."

"A full bag of Fullowag fills me full—I know! Wouldn't it be better to say *fills dogs* full of wags?"

"Say it like that."

Jill did so. Then Limpet said it. Then Jill again. Gradually they started laughing, for the words, spoken over and over again, began to lose their meaning.

"You're clever, Limpet," Jill said, all her bad temper leaving her at last. "We're sure to win. No one could think of anything better. I'm sure it's exactly what Brandy would say if he could."

"And it's better now it says *dogs* instead of *me*," said Limpet generously. "You'd better write it out on the paper. You write the best of us."

Brandy had to wait for his walk that day, for it took them nearly all the afternoon to guess all fifty dogs, to write the names neatly, to add the slogan, and to fill in names and addresses. They did it all in the trailer, borrowing Mrs. Remnant's pen which she had left behind.

"She won't mind when she hears what we needed it for," Jill said. "Just think—she doesn't even know about the island yet. She will be excited."

"What about Brandy?" Limpet said thoughtfully. "He can't tell us what he thinks about Fullowags—so how will he tell us whether he likes the island?"

"I suppose we shan't know till we get there."

"But if he doesn't like it—" Limpet began.

"Oh don't worry so much!" Jill cried. "I'm sure we can think of something. There's Aunt Katie—she's gone to live on the Isle of Wight. Perhaps we could go and see her and take Brandy—just to show him what an island's really like."

Once more Limpet was silent. You could almost see him thinking. He was thinking of something both easier and more daring than taking Brandy to Aunt Katie's new house on the Isle of Wight. But he decided to say nothing about it for the time being.

3

Preparations

Once their entry for the Fullowag contest was mailed, there was nothing for Jill and Limpet to do but be patient and wait for the results. These were to be announced on television, but not for several weeks. In the meantime, they talked endlessly about the island and made plans.

"I suppose there will be something more than trees," said Jill. "I don't suppose there'll be a proper house until we build one. But I guess there's a hut or something."

"We could live in that until the house was built," Limpet decided.

"It's very warm in the South Seas. If there wasn't room for everyone in the hut, Brandy and you and me could camp."

"In the South Seas it's the southern hemisphere, Jilly. That means the stars are upside down."

"And there will be coral reefs, with long waves breaking over them—"

"And sharks," said Limpet, cheerfully.

"But we shall swim in safe places."

"What do you think the island is called?"

They got out an atlas and found the right page after some difficulty, and they looked at the names of islands thereabouts. Some were hard to pronounce, some were quite easy. Some belonged to Britain, some to the United States, some to other countries. Some were tiny, nameless dots—perhaps one of those was their island.

When Mrs. Remnant returned from her short vacation, she had to be told at once what had been going on. Jill ran down to Little Paddock the moment she got home from school, and soon Limpet joined them. It was lovely to have Mrs. Remnant home and she was so glad to be back.

"I am very fond of my nephew, Jill—very fond indeed. But I cannot really get along with his wife. Just imagine—I might be living there until the end of my days but for you and dear Limpet and your kind parents letting me put a trailer in Little Paddock."

"It was all because of Brandy," Jill reminded her.

She and Mrs. Remnant hugged Brandy and told him how wonderful he was. He was used to admiration, but he looked a little surprised all the same.

Mrs. Remnant had brought Jill and Limpet and Brandy a present each. Brandy had a marrow bone, and that would have pleased him at any time. But Jill and Limpet had wonderful things, things that might have been chosen just for this moment in their lives. Limpet had a pocket compass; Jill had a magnifying glass.

"It's to read charts with!" she cried. "Oh, Mrs. Remnant—how did you know?"

Mrs. Remnant of course did not know anything, so without wasting any more time they began to tell her about the island, and about the contest for which it was the prize. They told her about naming the fifty dogs, the slogan that had had to be made up, and what their slogan was.

"No one could possibly have invented a better one," Jill said.

"Well," said Mrs. Remnant, frowning a little, "people can be very clever, you know."

"A full bag of Fullowag fills dogs full of wags. Don't you think it's the best slogan?"

"How can I tell? I don't know what the others are."

It was not like Mrs. Remnant to pour cold water on people's good ideas—perhaps she was tired after her journey.

"Mummy thinks it's good," Jill insisted. "So do Mr. and Mrs. Jeffreys—don't they, Limpet?"

Limpet nodded. He looked a little anxious. He

never expected things to be as easy as Jill thought they were—perhaps Mrs. Remnant felt the same?

"Well, well, we'll see," said Mrs. Remnant. "Brandy looks wonderful. You must have been looking after him very carefully indeed."

"And the parakeets," said Limpet.

"You must take them to the island, too," cried Jill. "I expect there'll be lots there—I expect they grow wild. It must be wonderful to see them flying about."

"Good gracious me," began Mrs. Remnant, and then said no more, as though she really could not find the words she wanted.

Jill not only thought about the island all the time, she talked about it all the time, too. It did not matter whether she was with Limpet or with her parents, there was nothing else that interested her.

One warm evening the Hyde family were sitting outside in the little garden that was all the ground that could be spared from the rows and rows of greenhouses. Jill's father, John Hyde, was reading a book about France.

"You know, dear," he said to his wife, "I think I could take some time off later in the summer. It would be nice if we could have a bit of a vacation together. I thought perhaps Mrs. Remnant would come and live in the house and look after Jill. And keep an eye on the nurseries for me. What do you think?"

"What a wonderful idea! I'm sure Mrs. Remnant would help. It's time you had a break."

Jill looked at her parents in amazement. "But the island—" she said.

"What about the island?" John Hyde asked.

"We shall have it by then. The results are on television in only a few weeks."

Her mother laughed a little at Jill's worried face. "Don't be *too* sure about winning it, will you, darling?"

Jill looked more worried than ever. "But you said you thought the slogan was awfully good. . . ."

"So I do. I do really. But just imagine the lots and lots of other people who must have thought of good ones, too."

"Oh, but I'm sure—" Jill began. Then she stopped. She could not help remembering how she had been sure about other things before—utterly, positively certain—and then had had to put up with a disappointment. For instance, how sure she had been that her parents would be delighted when she and Limpet had first brought Brandy home. And how very undelighted they were for a time, until Brandy proved himself a hero. But an island was different from a dog. She just would not believe that someone else, some stranger living in Manchester or Edinburgh or Cornwall might be the winner. "It'll be all right, you know," she said in a very firm, cheerful voice.

Mrs. Hyde looked at her husband. "Well anyway," she said at last, "even if you and Limpet win a South Sea island, Jill, that needn't stop Daddy and me from having a bit of a vacation."

"All right," said Jill, after some thought. "If we have to go off first—Limpet and me, I mean—I expect Mrs. Remnant would help us pack."

For the first time, her father began to look a bit annoyed.

"Do pull yourself together, Jill. You're old enough to know that things don't always happen the way you want them to."

"But sometimes they do, Daddy. This time could be one of the some."

"I give up," he said. "Margaret—see if you can get some sense into the child's head." And he went back, almost angrily, to his book.

Her mother looked at Jill. "Is Limpet sure about winning, too?"

"Of course he is!" But was he? For a second Jill wondered. He got excited about the affair when she did, but perhaps he was a shade less positive, rather more inclined to put questions into their conversation about the island. Where Jill said *We shall* do this or that, Limpet more often said *Shall we?* And he was the one who had thought about sharks. "He's *almost* sure Mummy."

"I think that's the best way to be, Jill. Otherwise it could be such a dreadful disappointment."

For a few hours after this, Jill felt quite moody and miserable. What was the matter with all the grown-ups? Why should it be so unlikely that she and Limpet would win the contest? Somebody had to—why not them? However, by the time she woke next morning, she was quite happy again. And when she met Limpet on the way to school, she had a new idea.

"You know what we ought to do—we ought to get in some supplies, Limpet."

"Do you mean for the island?"

"Yes, I do. I think we'd better make a list. You make a list and I'll make a list and then we'll make one together."

"All right," said Limpet. "Good idea. Toothpaste and things."

During the next few days the lists got longer and longer. Each evening when they met, Jill and Limpet compared notes. Sometimes the same thing turned up on both lists, but mostly they thought of different things. Jill put down potatoes and chocolate, pencils and paper, canned meat and tea and sewing thread. Limpet started with toothpaste and soap, brush and comb, which would have given anybody the idea that he was a particularly clean and tidy boy. After that he put down some very sensible things indeed—nails, a saw, a screwdriver, an oilcan, chewing gum, comics, candles, matches, flashlights and batteries.

After a bit they both began to feel rather as if they were not only going to the island, but were going to sail there, by themselves, on a raft.

"Now we know what we need, we must start collecting it all," Jill decided. "We can store the things in the shed—the one Brandy had for a kennel before he went back to live with Mrs. Remnant."

Brandy was with them at the time. Hearing his name, he got up slowly and shook himself, and padded around the table to Jill. He put his nose against her knee and blew.

"He wants a walk," said Limpet. "He doesn't understand about making lists."

"All right, let's take him. You go and tell Mrs. Remnant or she'll wonder where he is."

Limpet ran off. Jill put her arms around Brandy and hugged him.

"You'll never guess what we're planning," she said in his ear.

He flicked his ear and sighed. All he was bothered about was *now*. What about that walk?

Five minutes later, Jill and Limpet and Brandy were walking out of the wide gateway under the notice that read Hyde's Nursery Ltd.

"Downs or Windle Woods?" asked Limpet.

"Windle," said Jill. She was thinking hard. Now that
they had their list of supplies and a magnifying glass
and a compass, they really did need a little practical ex-
perience. Already they had discussed going to the Isle
of Wight to see Jill's Aunt Katie—but that had been
for Brandy's sake. It was only now that Jill thought
how much they needed to know themselves what it
felt like to be entirely surrounded by water. Windle

Woods, the lake, the island suddenly took up a very large part of Jill's imagination. "Limpet," she said, "about the Isle of Wight. It's a long way . . . and Aunt Katie might not understand . . . and I think if there was an island a bit nearer . . . well, we might see what that was like."

Limpet grinned. He started to run. He did not say that this was an idea he had had himself some time ago. He just dashed off toward Windle with Jill rushing after him. And Brandy who was as well aware as either of them that something exciting was going to happen came lumbering along quickly behind them.

4

Entirely
Surrounded by Water

It was about six o'clock. The woods were very quiet. The
evening sun in the clear sky made the water shine and
there was a thrush singing loudly in the top branch of
the one little tree on the island. Jill and Limpet and
Brandy came to the edge of the woods where the trees
were thin, and looked down the long grassy slope to the
lake. This was the place where they always stopped.
Never, never had they set so much as a toe on the grass
beyond. But this evening, Jill had decided, was to be
different.

She ran out on to the grass.

"Jilly—" called Limpet in a faint voice.

She went on down the slope. Limpet stood where he
was. Brandy went a few steps after Jill, turned and
came back to Limpet, then advanced again and waited
for him to follow.

"Coming," said Limpet—this time so faintly that no one else could have heard. He took the first faltering step away from the trees.

Then he was off. He ran down the grass after Jill and crashed into her where she stood on the edge of the water.

"About time," she said.

They stood together on the shore, Brandy close beside them. It was a very small lake and it looked quite shallow. There was a tangle of reeds at one end, and in the tangle something they had not noticed as they stood looking down from the end of the woods. There was a boat.

"Look," said Jill.

"Mm," said Limpet. He looked at her quickly, trying to see what she was thinking. "Better not," he said, when he saw her face.

Jill did not reply. It was only a few yards to the island. Goodness, you could almost jump it, if you were good at jumping and had extra-long legs. Or if you knew how to do a pole jump and had a pole—one leap and you would be there. You hardly needed a boat, except as a sort of bridge, the space between shore and shore looked so narrow.

"Come on," said Jill.

Without waiting to see if Limpet followed, she ran to the place where the boat lay among the reeds. Brandy came after her, then stopped and looked back.

He liked them to do the same things together and Limpet did not want to disappoint him, so he moved along the grass until he stood close to Jill.

"Someone might come. . . ."

"They won't. The boat's got some water in it," Jill said in a businesslike voice, "but not much."

Limpet edged a little closer, his hand on Brandy's collar as though he needed something to anchor him to the shore.

"Is it tied up?" he asked.

"The rope's just hanging in the water. That shows you."

Shows you what? Limpet wondered, but he did not say it out loud. Jill was pulling up the rope, and with it quantities of long, slimy weeds dripping with black mud. "Pooh—it's smelly," Limpet said.

"It'll be better when it gets into the air."

Jill wrinkled up her nose, but she went on pulling at the rope. Her hands were soon black and slithery and there were great drips of mud on her skirt, but this did not seem to worry her. At last the end of the rope appeared, and she gave it a tug. The boat moved slightly among the reeds that held it, and a slow ripple moved away from it, out and out across the water until it broke against the island shore.

"Oh look! Oh look!" Jill cried, pulling the rope harder, so that the boat twitched free of the reeds and floated toward them where they stood on the shore.

"It's got a bottom after all! It floats!" She had forgotten to talk quietly and was almost shouting in her excitement, so that Brandy began to bark and bound about like a puppy, and even Limpet forgot his fear that

someone might come and find them there. "Empty out
the water!" Jill cried.

She tugged the boat close to the edge of the lake, and
she and Limpet threw themselves down and began
splashing out the water with their hands. It went quite
surprisingly fast. Soon the boat was light enough to
rock delicately on the surface of the lake.

"No seats," said Limpet.

"We can sit on the bottom. It's nearly dry."

"No oars, Jilly."

"We can paddle with our hands—it's only a few
yards."

"Won't we get wet?"

"We can soon get dry again."

Limpet could not think of anything else that might
stop Jill getting into the boat, or stop him following
her. He had done his best and he could do no more.

"I'll go first," he said.

Jill did not argue about that—he was lighter than
she was, and it made sense to let him go and see what
happened when the boat felt his weight. She held the
boat as steady as possible, and very slowly and carefully
he put one foot over the edge.

"Look out, silly! You can't stand on one side of it!
It's tipping. . . ."

Limpet's first wish was to spring back onto dry land,
but pride forced him to jump the other way. He landed

in the boat all right, but it rocked so wildly that he hung on with both hands and turned quite pale.

"Are you all right?" Jill cried. "You can't be seasick, you know, because this isn't the sea. Look out—I'm coming!"

Now the boat was floating free on the water, and she must either get in quickly or be left behind. She hung on tightly and put one foot over the side. She felt the boat swing and bob. She knew she was going to over-balance. She hung on with every muscle she had, grinding her teeth together with the effort of keeping up-right. But the boat just went on its own way, and as Limpet grabbed her wrists she fell half in, half out, up to one knee in the oozy water. Somehow, as red in the face as Limpet was pale, she dragged her wet leg aboard. To do so, she had to give such a great heave and shove that she pushed the boat hard, and it went spinning and swaying out into the middle of the lake.

Jill picked herself up. She pushed her hair out of her eyes with her slime-covered hands. She was not going to admit that anything had gone wrong in the least bit.

"Nearly there!" she cried cheerfully.

Sure enough, the mainland was moving fast away from them, the island coming as quickly nearer. The lake was suddenly enormous, twice as big as it had seemed when they stood on the bank.

"Lovely!" cried Jill. "Isn't it lovely? Imagine it's the

Pacific Ocean! Imagine the sun's ten times hotter!"

"Imagine the sharks," said Limpet. "I think the water's coming in, Jilly."

"Bail it out, then."

"I can't bail and paddle at the same time."

"You bail. I'll paddle."

All this had made them so excited that they had forgotten Brandy. Now he lifted up his great head and howled to see them so far from him. The noise he made was terrible. If anything was likely to attract attention and bring somebody running, it was the sound of Brandy howling.

"We should have brought him with us, Limpet."

"He'd sink the boat."

"What shall we do? He's making such a din!"

"Go back and stop him, I suppose."

"I *must* get to the island now. We simply can't turn back."

She was right. They couldn't. When they tried to steer the boat it just went around in circles. More and more water came in, and they were soon sitting in an enormous puddle. The only good thing was that as they spun slowly and giddily across the water, the boat did move in the direction of the island.

"Perhaps there's a whirlpool," Limpet said. "That'd make it go around and around. . . ."

Jill ignored that. "The second we're near enough,

grab that bush," she ordered. "I'll keep on paddling as long as possible."

As she spoke, waves broke over the lake. The boat, which had seemed so nearly to have reached dry land, rocked wildly, and then spun away again into midstream.

"What's happened?" Jill cried.

"It's Brandy! He's swimming out to us! He's making great waves!"

Out he came, his chin held up out of the water as it streamed away over his shoulders from his huge paddling paws. He looked very like a white-haired old gentleman doing a steady length of the swimming pool. Even though they were getting wetter every minute,

Jill and Limpet broke out into wild laughter at the sight of him.

"Oh, isn't he wonderful! Oh, Brandy, you really are a dog and a half. . . . He'll be absolutely dripping, drenched."

"I'm drenched already," Limpet said.

"Not all down your back and over your shoulders like Brandy."

"Well, no . . ." began Limpet.

But at that second Brandy reached them. Grinning hugely, delighted with his own cleverness, sure of a welcome now as always, he put both his front paws on the edge of the boat. The water was shallow enough for him to stand up on his hind legs, and so his whole great weight dropped down hard on the boat. And the boat

simply broke up. The bottom fell out and the remain-
der kicked up in the air before gurgling to the bottom,
hurling Jill and Limpet into a mess of mud and weeds
and dreadfully cold water. It was just deep enough for
them to go right under and then come scrambling up
again gasping and spluttering.

Brandy had never seen anything quite so funny.
This was the best game he had ever had. He had never
enjoyed anything so much as this frolicking with two
friends in such a vast amount of lovely, splashy water.
No sooner were they up than he slapped them down
again, a loving grin all over his dripping face. He nuz-
zled and nibbled at them and would not let them catch
hold of him. As they yelled at him to stop, to let them
go, to be sensible, as he splashed and barked around

them, the noise echoed in the quiet evening, over the water, over the island, over the woods and far beyond. Only when they both managed to grab his collar at the same moment, and to hang on to it, did he agree that the game might perhaps have gone on long enough.

Their struggling had carried them away from the island and nearer to the shore. Brandy pulled them the last few yards and they let him go as he bounded forward to dry land, shaking himself enormously and adding a few more drips to the weight of muddy water that ran and oozed from their clothes and their hair and their noses and their eyes as they waded after him.

The joke was over, the game was at an end. What was going to happen now? What in the world were their parents going to say when they reached home? And anyway how were they going to get home? It meant running through the village dripping wet and plastered with mud and misery.

At this horrible moment they heard shouting.

An old gentleman was running toward the lake from the direction of the house. His hair was white, his face was red. He carried a thick stick which he shook in fury as he came.

"Mr. Tapsell," said Limpet, only just above a whisper, and for a second he looked as though he wanted to plunge into the water again and swim back to the island for safety.

5

Mr. Tapsell
and Miss Tapsell

Mr. Tapsell was short and sturdy and his white hair was rather long, so that it waved in the breeze as he rushed toward them.

"Look out," said Jill. And she grabbed Limpet and actually turned back until she was standing in the water up to her knees. Brandy leaped after them.

"Come out of there! Come out, I say! You're trespassing on my property! Just let me get my hands on you!"

"As if we would," said Jill to Limpet. "Oh—*what* shall we do?"

"What *can* we do? We're caught."

"Get a move on there!" old Mr. Tapsell was shouting in his rather thin but very angry voice. And he banged his stick on the ground.

47

Brandy was the first one out of the water. He was wet again, so he had to shake himself. It did not help matters that he shook himself all over Mr. Tapsell's trousers.

"Confound the beast—he's drenched me! You abominable children—how dare you come here upsetting me!"

Limpet, then Jill, struggled out of the squelching mud. If only, as Brandy did now, they could have rolled on the grass and dried themselves a bit. They moved slowly toward Mr. Tapsell and stood in front of him, side by side, like prisoners in front of a judge.

"Well? What have you to say? Explain yourselves, please."

What was there to explain? Anyone could see that they had taken the boat, fallen in the water, and been caught.

"We just wanted to see what the island was like."

"Just wanted to see, indeed! Well—and have you seen? And has it done you any good?"

"No, sir," Limpet replied, very politely.

"No, indeed, it's done you harm. See what comes of trespassing. You know, of course, that this is a matter for the police? And you," he said to Jill, "you're older than your brother and should know better than to lead him into mischief."

"He's not my brother, Mr. Tapsell," said Jill.

The old gentleman started slightly and peered at

her. "Know m'name, do you?" He peered still closer, as though trying to see Jill through her coating of mud. "Bless me—are you John Hyde's girl? Haven't I seen you at Hyde's Nursery?"

"Yes, I'm Jill Hyde. And this is Limpet Jeffreys. His name's Lambert really."

"Jeffreys? Jeffreys? Related to the butcher?"

Limpet nodded furiously and the water sprayed out from his hair almost as it had sprayed out from Brandy's great, thick coat.

"Of course. Yes, of course. Now I recall that enormous dog." He looked at the three of them, for Brandy had now joined the line and was beginning to look somewhat calmer. Limpet said afterward that Mr. Tapsell probably decided then that he might get very tough joints for his Sunday dinners if he reported the butcher's only son to the police. "Hm," he went on. "Well. Well, we'll see."

It was at this moment that Jill gave a tremendous shiver. The sun had gone down behind the trees and she was very, very wet. She tried to squeeze the water out of her skirt, and suddenly she was so miserable she did not know what to do with herself. She turned away and put her arms around Brandy. He was wet, too, but it did not seem to worry him—but he knew at once how she was feeling, for he licked her face lovingly.

"Oh dear," said Mr. Tapsell, "I'm afraid you're catching a cold. Oh dear! Oh dear me! Perhaps I have

been hasty." He made a little tutting noise that was suddenly quite friendly. "Come to the house," he decided. "Come now. We must dry you before you go home. Oh my goodness me, what in the world are your parents going to say if they see you like that?" He began flapping his hands and waving his stick at them. "Now," he cried. "Now—fall into line. Follow me. Walk briskly and you will keep warm. Right, now— right turn and quick, very quick march!"

Swinging his stick, he turned smartly. Limpet fell into step behind him, Jill behind Limpet, Brandy behind Jill. The marching column went briskly across the grass, through some trees, along by the summer house, through a thick shrubbery, and across a fine lawn toward the open French windows of the sitting room. There sat Miss Tapsell with her needlework fallen into her lap and her mouth open in astonishment at the extraordinary sight that was approaching across the lawn.

"Connie!" called Mr. Tapsell. "Disaster! An accident! Your help is needed. These unhappy children have nearly drowned themselves in the lake."

Hearing themselves changed from *abominable* children to *unhappy* ones, Jill and Limpet knew at once that the worst of their troubles was over. Mr. Tapsell's anger had all gone out of him. His only care now was to get them clean and dry again.

Without a thought for the beautiful carpet, Miss

Tapsell drew them indoors—Brandy, too—and she knew at once how best to deal with the matter.

"Hot baths," she decided. "Not a moment to waste. Walter—go and turn on the taps in the bathroom. That's for you, my dear," she said to Jill. "You," she told Limpet, "must make do with the scullery sink— it's huge and the water's bubbling. And as for you," she said to Brandy, "you'll just have to dry yourself in front of the kitchen fire."

Within seconds it seemed that the whole house was being turned upside down. Water ran and gushed and steamed. Hot towels were snatched from the airing cupboard. Clean clothes were turned out of drawers and wardrobes. It seemed hardly possible that the misery of a few minutes before could so quickly have turned into such kindness. What had happened to make things so very different from what might have been expected? Where was the alarming Mr. Tapsell now, the forbidding Miss Tapsell? As Miss Tapsell dashed about her face turned from pale pink to bright pink then to red, her hair grew more and more untidy. But anybody could see that she was enjoying herself. It was as though she had been waiting for years for just such an occasion as this, Jill thought, as she lay in the enormous bathtub and cleaned the mud off, and grew warm and comfortable again.

Both Mr. and Miss Tapsell, though they were short, were fat. Their clothes were all they could offer the two guests and the result was very extraordinary, indeed. Jill wore a skirt that trailed around her ankles, a blouse with flapping sleeves, shoes that slopped as she walked —and a towel wound around her wet hair.

"You look exactly right," Miss Tapsell told her. "Now come down to the kitchen, for I must make you a drink to warm you inside as well as out."

Limpet was in the kitchen already, with Brandy and Mr. Tapsell. He was wearing an ancient pair of pants that came down to his ankles, where they were tied with shoelaces, and a huge sweater with a hole in it. The neck came down so low on his chest that Mr. Tapsell had bundled a woolen scarf around him and tied it in a knot.

"I'm stifled," cried poor Limpet. "I'll die of heat! Oh, must I wear the scarf?"

"Certainly. Cover your chest, my boy. You'll get bronchitis if you don't. Isn't that so, Connie?"

"Something thinner," she said—and handed him a silk scarf of her own, which he had to put on, though it was covered with roses.

On the table two silver mugs stood side by side. On the stove a saucepan bubbled. The hot drink Miss Tapsell was making smelled rather strange. Every so often she pulled down one of a long row of jars that stood on a shelf above the stove, took out a pinch of the contents and threw that pinch into the saucepan—like a witch making a magic brew.

"I used to make this for my poor father, when he had one of his chills," Miss Tapsell said. "My poor mother gave me the recipe. She was given it by my poor grandmother."

She did not say why they were all so poor. Jill thought of all she had heard about old Mr. Tapsell. *His poor family,* she said to herself.

Suddenly Miss Tapsell threw a pinch of something fresh into the saucepan. The mixture frothed and sizzled, and she instantly became very excited, pouring the liquid into the mugs and crying—"Quick! Quick! Pour it while it's frothing; drink it while it's hot. That's what we always say in this house."

To their surprise, the drink was delicious. It tasted of oranges and sugar and mysterious spices, and it went down in a wonderful glowing stream of warmth that seemed to reach their very toes and heels. Brandy watched them, his tail slowly waving, his tongue lolling out.

"Look out!" cried Jill. "He's going to dribble. Is there even a drop left in the saucepan for him?"

There was enough to cover a large saucer, and Brandy lapped it up.

"There," said Miss Tapsell, as she and her brother watched the guests. "Look at them, Walter. Their cheeks are beginning to glow."

"Just as they should," he agreed. He smiled in a satisfied way at Jill and Limpet. "First you fell into the lake," he said, "and now you have fallen into good hands." He seemed to have forgotten that he had ever been angry.

"But how did you come to be in the lake at all?" asked Miss Tapsell for the first time.

So sitting there in the warmth, in their strange clothes, Jill and Limpet explained about Fullowag, and the contest, and how they had wanted so badly to find out exactly what an island was like.

"But we never found out after all," Jill said, beginning to think of all the things that had happened and that had not happened. "And we broke the boat."

"It was broken years ago," Mr. Tapsell said. "We are not worried about that. But we are worried that you might have been drowned."

"Oh, but it's so shallow," Jill cried.

"We could almost have crawled to the island," Limpet said.

"Ah yes, it seems very shallow," Mr. Tapsell agreed, shaking his head.

"But there's a treacherous hole, you see," his sister said. "And unless you know where it is, you could indeed drown."

"That is why there are so many notices telling people to keep out," said Mr. Tapsell. "But the fence is very broken now, I know. I am afraid, Connie, we must go to the expense of putting up a new one."

"Or," said Limpet quickly, "you could fill up the hole in the lake."

"Fill it up?" Mr. Tapsell looked from Limpet to Miss Tapsell in amazement. " 'Fill it up,' he says, Connie. That is a remarkably sound idea. We should have thought of it years ago. How would we set about it, do you think?"

"Stones," said Limpet, sitting on the edge of his chair with his hands on his knees, and looking in his borrowed clothes like some sort of gnome. "Loads of stones. Collected in a heap. Thrown in."

"*We* could collect the stones!" Jill cried. "We could make a huge pile of them—a mound, a whole mound. And then throw them in," she added, seeing that this would be the best part of the business.

"And Brandy would help," said Limpet. "Once Mrs. Remnant was going to get him a little cart—he's quite big enough to pull one, and he is very obliging. My father knows how to make little carts."

"Mrs. Remnant would be pleased, too," Jill said. "She's always worrying that Brandy doesn't get enough exercise."

Mr. Tapsell was silent; Miss Tapsell was silent. Then first one, and then the other, took out a handkerchief—one huge, one tiny—and blew their noses hard.

"So you'll come again," Miss Tapsell said.

"Yes, *please!*"

"We should like that . . . so few friends . . . no visitors . . . so fond of young people . . ." murmured Miss Tapsell into her hanky.

"We are very out of the way here," Mr. Tapsell explained, as he recovered himself. "My sister means we often feel too quiet altogether. It was how we were brought up, you know . . . strictly . . . not expected to need a lot of amusements. . . . Well, the truth is, once people find you unfriendly, as they suppose, they never give you a chance to explain."

"So—yes, yes!" Miss Tapsell cried. "Please come as often as you can and collect all the stones you need. We shall be so happy to see you here." The time was now going fast, and both Jill and Limpet were very much aware that they would have to go home. But their own clothes were not nearly dry. Either they must walk home through the village wearing their borrowed things, or they must get one of their fathers to come and fetch them. It was difficult to decide which would be worse—it was even difficult to decide which father would be worse.

Mr. Tapsell decided for them. "I shall telephone Hyde's Nursery now," he said. And he was out of the room before they could even think how to reply.

It took John Hyde about five minutes to jump in the truck and drive around to Windle Lodge. Jill heard the wheels scrunching on the drive and her heart bumped. She could tell by the way her father braked that he was angry—he let the brake click loudly instead of pulling it up without any sound. She knew it again by his quick step up to the door, even by the way he rang the bell. She looked at Limpet. He knew, too. He would never say *It was all your fault,* because he was not that kind of friend—but she knew whose fault it was. She had bossed him as usual and now they were in trouble.

Mr. Tapsell was opening the door, Jill's father was striding into the house. Snatches of unpromising conversation could be heard—old enough to know better, need a good talking to, and so on.

"Daddy," said Jill quickly, as he strode into the room, "we fell in."

There she stood with Limpet beside her, Brandy, uneasy, hiding himself behind them, finding plenty of cover in the long skirt and the big hairy pants. Jill saw her father's hand fly to his face at the picture they made, but if there was a smile there he wiped it away very quickly indeed.

"If you have said how sorry you are, you had better get in the truck as quickly as possible," he said sternly.

It was a miserable ending, and they slunk out like criminals. Mr. Tapsell and his sister stood side by side on the step as the truck drove away. Jill looked back. The two old people were still there. Miss Tapsell waved gently, just once, then quickly put her hand behind her back.

"They didn't mind, Daddy," Jill said. "They didn't mind one bit."

"We'll soon know about that. I shan't be at all surprised if Mr. Tapsell cancels his order for roses. Anyone knows he's a difficult chap—"

"But he isn't—he isn't!" cried Jill.

"Be quiet, Jill. I know what I'm talking about. How can I expect him to believe I can look after plants, when I can't even look after my own daughter and keep her out of mischief?"

"It was the island. We wanted to try it. We wanted to know what it's like being in the middle of a lot of water."

Jill's father would stand a lot with great patience—as he had done once over Brandy—but when he decided he had had enough, then there could be no doubt about his feelings.

"Island! Island! I'm sick of hearing the word! From now on it's not to be used in my hearing—is that clear? I don't want to hear anything more about the contest or the South Seas or Fullowag or anything remotely to do with it. Understand that, please. I've said it before and I'll say it again—the sooner you grow up a bit, Jill, and learn that things just cannot always go the way you want them to—then the easier it's going to be for all of us."

Jill did not answer. She was sitting on the floor of the truck with Limpet leaning against her and Brandy

close by. Limpet moved a bit nearer. Brandy gave one
of his sighs. He laid his chin thoughtfully on the horrid
bundle of wet muddy clothes, a fine collection of wash-
ing for two long-suffering mothers to deal with.

6

A Hole in the Water

When Jill woke next morning, she lay still, knowing that something had gone wrong but unable to remember at first what it was. The morning was fine. Turning her head toward the window, she saw blue sky, trees, birds flying—spring was well advanced now and they were too busy finding nesting material to idle about in the branches singing at this time of day. And then, on a chair near the window, Jill saw clothes that were certainly not hers. She saw a skirt, a blouse, shoes. . . . She remembered what had happened yesterday evening.

Even Jill's mother, who took things very easily as a rule, had been angry about all that falling in the lake.

"What a crazy thing to do!" she had cried. "Anyone knows the lake at Windle is dangerous."

"We didn't know."

"Why do you suppose there are all those notices about Private and Trespassers Will Be Prosecuted?"

"Why don't they say Dangerous Lake? Then there'd be some sense in it."

"Don't argue with me, Jill. If there's a notice saying Private, that ought to be enough. You had no business to be in the woods, let alone right down by the lake."

Jill had decided not to explain any more why she and Limpet had needed to see what an island was like. She was afraid her mother might grow as furious as her father had. . . .

She thought about the island now as she lay in bed. It was quite a long while before she realized that the island she was thinking about was not the one in the South Seas at all, but the one in Windle Lake on which they had failed to land their leaking boat. Of course it was much too small to live on, and there was not likely to be endless sunshine. But what a dear little island it had seemed as they floated near to it, and how sad and angry she felt that they had not been able to set foot there after all. The boat was broken, so how would they ever get there? Now that they knew Mr. Tapsell and Miss Tapsell and liked them so much, they could not possibly go on their land without asking permission. That permission would not be given, she felt certain, while the dangerous hole existed. Limpet had been right; the hole must be filled.

As usual, he was waiting to walk to school with Jill. He was standing by the gate, looking rather small and thin, which always happened when he was unhappy. His mother and father must have been furious with him—his father, anyway; his mother was not the furious sort.

"Did you ask about the cart?" Jill asked, as they set off together.

"What cart?"

"For Brandy, of course. For the stones. To fill the hole. The hole in the water."

"You can't have a hole in water."

"Of course you can. That's where they think we'll drown."

"But the hole's not in the *water*."

"It's in the lake. That's water, isn't it?"

"The hole's in the ground and the lake's on top of it."

"I don't care!" shouted Jill. "It's got to be filled with stones!"

They both stayed at school for lunch, so there was plenty of time to be friends again before they reached home that afternoon. Limpet said he would ask his father about the cart; Jill said she would find Mrs. Remnant and make sure she would not mind if Brandy helped with the stones. After tea they would meet by the gate to Hyde's Nursery and tell one another what had happened.

Mrs. Remnant was gardening when Jill reached the trailer. The whole of Little Paddock was her garden, and it was planted with things that liked to grow in grass or to ramble over hedges. Mrs. Remnant was trying to help some honeysuckle up into a tree when Jill arrived. Brandy was lying in the shade, for the evening was warm. He did not get up, but just moved his tail slightly. She had the feeling that he was as much in disgrace as she was.

"Did he take long to dry, Mrs. Remnant?"

"Quite long enough. I shall have to think twice

about letting him go out with you and Limpet, if you let him get up to such silly pranks."

"But he did enjoy it, Mrs. Remnant."

"I daresay he did. But I didn't enjoy getting the mud out of his coat."

Jill sighed. All the grown-ups seemed to have been upset by yesterday's adventure, perhaps because they knew it had its dangers, however well it had turned out in the end. This was clearly quite the wrong moment for asking Mrs. Remnant if they could harness Brandy to a little cart, but Jill could not stop herself. Out came the tale about filling up the dangerous hole with stones.

"Why bother?" asked Mrs. Remnant.

"Well—because then they might let us borrow a boat or something, and go on the lake again, and get to the island."

"I thought you were going off to the South Seas, Jill? You don't need an island there *and* an island here, surely?"

"But in case anything went wrong," Jill said slowly, "and somebody else won the contest after all. . . ." Somehow, since yesterday, she was readier to see that things do not always work out precisely as planned.

Mrs. Remnant turned back to her gardening, and when next she spoke, it was without looking at Jill.

"Just in case, then," she agreed. "All right. He won't mind, I know. But remember not to overwork him."

Jill felt better at once. She raced off, shouting her thanks.

Limpet was waiting by the gate.

"He won't do it," he said.

"Why not? What did he say?"

"He says he knows how to make a little cart, but he doesn't know how to make time." Limpet sighed. "He means he's too busy."

"I know what he means," Jill said. Privately, she could not believe Mr. Jeffreys was too busy for such an important job; she felt he just wouldn't help.

Limpet sat down on the grass bank by the gate, and Jill swung on the gate, trying to think how else to arrange things. There was a shed nearby where things that might come in handy one day were stored. Among them were some baskets of the kind that new potatoes are packed in.

"There you are," said Jill. "I knew there'd be some other way. We can fasten the baskets one on either side of Brandy. Donkeys have them sometimes. I've seen pictures."

"How do you fix them?"

"I don't know. But we can easily find out," said Jill.

At this moment, her mother came to the door of the house and called to her.

"What about those clothes of Miss Tapsell's? You'd better take them back. I'll put them in a bag for you. What about yours, Limpet?"

Limpet mumbled, "My Dad took them. He went to say he was sorry, so he took them with him."

He looked so miserable that Jill's mother laughed. "Cheer up," she said. "I daresay we'll all forgive you quite soon. But do try to be more sensible in the future. Now—why don't you run and fetch Brandy, then you can all walk down to Windle Lodge and *you* can say you're sorry."

Jill and Limpet went off at once in the direction of Little Paddock. They knew that the business of falling in the lake was over now. They would have no difficulty in saying they were sorry for their new friends were not even angry. It was quite strange to recall that when they first saw Mr. Tapsell coming toward them shouting, they had wanted so much to run away.

It was strange, too, to go all around the boundary of the Tapsells' property and to walk up to the front door of Windle Lodge. But today they were proper visitors, instead of trespassers sneaking over ground which was really forbidden to them.

"We have come to make arrangements about the stones," Jill explained, when they had once more apologized for having given so much trouble. "We can't get a little cart, but we are going to hang two baskets across Brandy's back, so that he can help. We'll soon fill up the hole for you."

"Ah—the hole," said Mr. Tapsell. "You are going to fill it up—you can really do that for us, you think?

Come here, Connie, and listen to this. Now isn't this an excellent idea? These three young people are going to collect stones and fill up the hole in the lake."

"Only Brandy isn't really a young person," Limpet said.

"He's eight years old—and that means forty-six in human age," Jill explained. "But he's very strong, and Mrs. Remnant thinks it's all right."

"Why didn't we think of this years ago?" Miss Tapsell cried. "Then we needn't have put up so many notices, and then people might not have been so unfriendly."

"But you didn't put up the notices," Jill reminded her. "It was your father, wasn't it?"

"Yes, it was Papa," agreed Miss Tapsell. "Perhaps he knew it would keep away friends as well as enemies. He was not a very friendly man. Poor Papa."

They all sat down and discussed how best to set about the business of filling in the hole. Everyone seemed to know the hole was a large one, but there were lots of stone in the woods, where there was a small quarry.

"You must be careful, though," Miss Tapsell said. "Please don't try to move anything too large for you. We rely on you to be sensible."

Naturally Jill and Limpet agreed that they would be sensible, and by the time they left, all the plans had been made. They looked back as they went through the gates of Windle and saw Mr. Tapsell and his sister roaring with laughter.

"I hope they're not laughing at us, Jilly. . . ."

"Of course not. Why should they be? They're pleased, that's all," Jill decided.

Whatever Jill did, she did with all her might—whether it was planning to go and live with her whole family in the South Seas or collecting stones to fill an invisible hole of unknown size. And since whatever she did Limpet did, too, their families now began to hear almost as much about the stones and the hole and Windle Lake, as they had heard about Fullowag and palm trees and sunshine.

"You seem to be quite an expert at the job," Jill's father said to her. "When you've finished the hole, you can collect some stones for me. I've always wanted to build a wall."

"Oh, but by that time—" began Jill. But she did not finish what she had been going to say, since he had absolutely forbidden her to mention certain matters in his presence. *By that time,* she had been going to say, *we shall have the results of the contest.* . . . She glanced quickly at her father to see if he had noticed anything. He was going through some orders that had come by mail, but he had stopped to look at her. He was not quite smiling. He looked as though he would very much like to know what she was thinking about.

The whole business of the stones and Windle and

the Tapsells had come at exactly the right moment. Even Jill could think of nothing more to do in preparation for a move to the South Seas, for although the supplies were only on a list they had not anything like enough money to buy them. And anyway, there was just the chance, as Jill had now begun to admit, that something might go wrong. How foolish they would look if they had a shed full of canned meat and prunes and flashlight batteries—and no island to sail to. They had needed the distraction of something absolutely new to help them through the last days of waiting— and here it was. It was not only a hole that was being filled in, but time as well.

Each day after school, Jill and Limpet and Brandy went rushing to Windle. They had not found a way of fastening the baskets on Brandy's back, but he helped in other ways—he would always bound about barking in a cheerful manner if they got a bit tired of lugging their loads to the lake shore. At first they filled the baskets with stones and dragged them over the ground to the spot where the hole was marked by one very rotten pole. But they soon found other ways. They piled stones on a square of wire netting and dragged it with two lengths of rope they found in a shed. In the same place they found an ancient roll of linoleum, and they stuffed the stones into the roll and sent the whole thing bowling down the slope. This was best of all until the linoleum gathered so much speed that it shot into the

air as it reached the lake and then dropped into the water, sinking without a trace.

"The hole must be huge," Jill decided. "We shall need twice as many stones as we've got already."

Collecting stones into a great mound might seem a tedious business, but their new friendship with Mr. Tapsell and his sister made it a wonderful entertainment that they did not want to end. There were cookies and lemonade each evening before they went home, or perhaps ice cream or fruit salad with Miss Tapsell's homemade sponge cake. The very thought of the Tapsells filled Jill and Limpet with pride, for of all the village only they knew how kind and generous brother and sister truly were.

At last there was such a huge mound of stones that it looked big enough to fill in the entire lake. The gardener was to help with the actual filling of the hole, and however reluctantly, Jill and Limpet had promised not to throw in any stones unless he was there. But it was difficult to get Mr. Tapsell to decide when the actual filling of the hole should take place. Whenever they asked him, he put them off. Once he even said the gardener was away from work with a bad back—but they had already seen him mowing the lawn as they passed on the way home from school.

"We don't need any more stones, Mr. Tapsell," Jill said at last. "Couldn't we fill up the hole on Saturday?"

"Well—perhaps. Yes, perhaps Sunday," he said vaguely.

"No, no, Walter—not Saturday!" cried Miss Tapsell. She frowned at her brother, and shook her head.

"No, no—of course not. Silly of me. Not Saturday," agreed Mr. Tapsell. And then he said, in a voice unlike any he had used before to Jill or Limpet, "We'll let you know. That would be best. Wouldn't it, Connie?"

"Yes. We'll telephone. We'll ring you up when the gardener's well again."

Jill and Limpet walked home from Windle rather slowly, and for a long time neither of them spoke. Something had happened, or was about to happen, that they did not understand. But as they went along together they remembered all the tales they had heard of the "difficulty" of Mr. Tapsell and his sister.

"Do you think they just wanted someone to collect stones for them?" Jill said at last.

"I don't know, Jilly."

They went on for some way without speaking, then Jill said, "Well, I don't care. It's only a week to the Fullowag results. We shan't need to bother with a lot of old stones and the old Tapsells after that."

Limpet did not answer. He seemed dreadfully downcast. It was difficult to tell whether he was more unhappy about the behavior of their new friends, or about the coming results of the contest.

When Saturday morning came, Jill wandered off in the direction of Windle, without actually saying she was going. Limpet came after her, and Brandy came after both. Perhaps by now the gardener would be better, the Tapsells in a more comfortable mood. . . .

"Just look around the bushes and see if you can see anyone," Jill ordered Limpet, when they reached the gate.

He squeezed along the edge of the shrubbery, yard by yard, until he could see the house.

Then he called out to her—"Jilly! Jilly, look! Quick!"

She ran to his side and gazed with him at the front of the house. The door was tightly closed and so was every window. On the ground floor, all the curtains were pulled.

"They've gone away, Limpet! Why didn't they say they were going? Oh—oh, what can have happened?"

7

Keep Out. Strictly Private

"Perhaps they're in the kitchen," Limpet said.

Although it was perfectly clear that they were no-where about the place, Jill was as anxious as Limpet to put off admitting this. She ran through the shrubbery that cut off the front part of the house and garden from the back, with Limpet and Brandy following her closely. For the first time they discovered that the shrubs concealed a fence. For the first time a door that must always have stood open, was not only closed but locked against them.

This time it was Limpet who insisted on looking on the bright side. He said they would certainly be back soon.

"Why didn't they say they were going, then?"

"Because they'll be back soon," he replied.

"People don't lock up and pull their curtains when they're coming back soon."

They began walking away from the locked door. They went back through the shrubbery and stood uncertainly by the front door. They sat down on the step and tried to understand what could have happened to make their new friends behave so strangely. They felt almost tricked, and both remembered how Miss Tapsell had said *No, no—not Saturday,* and how their manner had been quite changed.

"As though they were hiding something," Jill said slowly. "As though they knew something we didn't know. . . ." And suddenly she became quite wild in her manner, as only Jill could. "We should never have told them about Fullowag!" she cried.

"Why ever not? What's Fullowag got to do with it?"

"Can't you see? We never should have given them the idea. They must have rushed out and got a form and gone in for the contest themselves. I bet they used our slogan! And what's more," cried Jill, growing sillier and sillier, "they kept us collecting stones so that we wouldn't find out. And do you know where they are now? They're in the South Seas! Because they've won the island. They've won our island!"

Limpet sighed and said in a flat firm voice—"That's jolly clever of them. The contest ended weeks ago. Why—we only just managed to do it in time. And the results aren't till next Saturday, anyway."

"Perhaps they know the manager. . . ! Perhaps we muddled the dates. . . !"

"I wish we had!" Limpet almost shouted. "I don't want to win your old island. I'm sick of it. I don't want to go to the South Seas—I like it here. I'm not coming, even if we win. You can keep the lot and good luck to you. I'm fed up. Go to your old South Seas. Brandy and I can manage without you."

By the time Limpet had got to the end of this un-Limpet-like speech, he was stamping away down the drive shouting the last words over his shoulder.

Jill sprang to her feet. "Come back!" she commanded.

Limpet's only answer was to whistle and snap his fingers at Brandy. Brandy bounded forward. Jill grabbed at his collar, missed and went down on one knee. Limpet whistled again and Brandy reached his side. Jill tried to whistle, but she was in such a state she had not enough breath. She called instead—"Brandy!"

He stopped and looked back. He turned slightly, moved a little toward her, then stood waiting.

"Brandy!" cried Limpet.

"Brandy!" cried Jill.

For a few seconds, Brandy thought this was some lovely new game, and he hurled himself backward and forward from one to the other until he was giddy. Then he sat down halfway between the two of them and refused to budge.

"One of us has got to take him home," Jill said.

"Stop calling him, then, and I will."

"I don't know what's happened to you, Limpet. You sound like a different person."

"Hm," said Limpet, looking rather pleased.

"It's not a good day to quarrel," Jill said fussily.

"We've got too much to think about and we've just got to think about it together." She could feel herself beginning to say she was sorry. She could not bear to have a real quarrel with Limpet—little ones didn't matter, but this was serious. But it was so difficult suddenly to change, when she was used to ordering him about.

He was moving on again. If he left her and went home, with or without Brandy, it would be ten times more difficult to make up their difference.

She called after him, trying to sound friendly. "I didn't really mean it about Fullowag. It was a joke."

It was not really good enough, but Limpet seemed to decide it would have to do. He stopped and looked back.

"I'm going up to the woods. We can get in that way, in case they're hiding somewhere—perhaps *they're* only joking, too. Are you coming?"

Jill ran after him.

It was almost half a mile around the edge of Windle to the woods on the slope above the lake. Limpet led the way, Jill followed, Brandy shifted from the front to the back of this column of two, rather as though they were sheep and he was the dog who had the job of herding them to the right place. It must have seemed rather strange to him to see Limpet ahead and Jill behind, for it had never happened that way in all the time he had known them. There was also the unusual fact that instead of talking the whole time, Jill and

Limpet walked in silence. Only when they came within yards of the woods was the silence broken. It was broken by cries of dismay.

"Oh what's happened? What are they doing?"

"They're putting up a new fence."

"Not only a fence. . . ."

"New notices, Jilly. . . ."

With rolls of wire and bundles of thick stakes, three men were working away at enclosing the Windle woodland. A fourth had taken down a number of the old notices and was busily replacing them with new. STRICTLY PRIVATE had taken the place of the milder PRIVATE. But worst of all was a whole pile of those waiting to be put up.

"Ask them," Limpet said. "Ask them what they're doing."

"You ask them."

It would have been easy if the men had belonged to the village, but they were all strangers. This made the whole situation seem much worse—as though some enemy had come to seize the place and rule it.

Jill gave Limpet a push and they moved together toward the men. Then they stopped and stood watching, for what were they to ask? It would be foolish to say *What are you doing?* for the answer was all too plain. *Why are you doing it?* would be as bad. They were doing it because they had been told to, because it was their job and they would be paid for it. As for who

would pay them, there could be no doubt about that, either.

By now the men had noticed that they were being watched. One of them called out and asked what Jill and Limpet wanted.

"Did Mr. Tapsell tell you to do that?" Limpet asked.

"It was the boss told us, mate," came the reply. "Can't say who told the boss."

"Tapsell?" said the second. "That's the name. Mr. Tapsell of Windle Lodge. This is Windle Wood, isn't it? So that makes sense."

"Mr. Tapsell's gone away," Jill said. "Did he say where he was going?"

"Couldn't say, dear. Never spoke to him."

"Well—did they say to you—I mean, did the boss say to get it finished while Mr. Tapsell was away?"

"Come to think of it, he did say something. 'Get it done quickly,' he said. 'So's the old boy'll find it all done by the time he comes home.' "

Jill looked at Limpet and they moved a few steps away.

"We shall never be able to come here again," she said. "We collected all those stones for nothing. And we haven't got any new friends after all. Daddy did say," she remembered, "that Mr. Tapsell was a difficult sort of chap."

"Now then," called the head workman, "you two

buzz along out of it. This is no place for kids. Don't let me have to get tough with you."

As they walked away, they heard the men laughing, and the quick sharp sound of hammer and nails as another KEEP OUT notice went up into its place.

8

A Letter from Fullowag

Jill had, of course, made no mistake about the date, and the results of the Fullowag contest were to be announced in a special program on the following Saturday. Apart from the dreadful strain of waiting, and of getting through these last few days, Jill was much concerned with the strange and disappointing behavior of the Tapsells. Then there was the matter of Limpet— she would have to stop ordering him about so much or she would find herself without her most important friend. So she had a lot to worry about, in one way and another.

"If only they had *said* they were going away," Jill complained to her mother.

"They always go for a short vacation at this time of year."

"How do you know?"

"Miss Tapsell told me so."

"When did she tell you so? I thought you only just knew her."

"Just knowing someone is knowing them enough to know that much," replied her mother in a confused and rather flustered way that made Jill look at her in surprise. "Anyway, Jill, do try to be more cheerful. You know we've got Aunt Katie here for a few days—don't let her find you moping."

Jill had forgotten and the news merely added to her troubles. Aunt Katie was her mother's sister, but they could not have been less alike. Getting through this week was going to be bad enough, without the added trouble of having Aunt Katie as a guest in the house; she was such a disapproving sort of person. The only hope was that she could hardly fail to know about islands, and she must at least have lots to tell about the Isle of Wight and about the strangeness of being cut off from the mainland with only a boat to join you to the rest of England.

"Is it your own boat?" she asked the visitor, on the evening of her arrival.

"Is what my own boat, Jill? That question doesn't really make sense, does it?"

"I mean the one you go to England in. Do you have to sail it yourself and go shopping in it and everything?"

"My dear child, I may live on an island now, but it is still part of England. The Isle of Wight is quite a big place. It has towns and villages of its own. When I go shopping, I take a basket to the town, like everyone else."

As most often when talking to her aunt, Jill was made to feel very small and silly.

"But tell me about it," she said, trying again.

"Tell you about the island? I don't think there's anything to tell."

John Hyde had just come in and was standing listening. "I'll take you there one day, Jill," he said. She knew he felt sorry for her, because Aunt Katie had really been very snubbing. And as though he wanted to help her over the difficult moment, he forgot he had forbidden the mention of a certain subject. "Jill's mad about islands," he told his sister-in-law. "She nearly drowned herself trying to cross a lake to one. She and Limpet went in a boat without a bottom."

"Nearly drowned herself? John—how can you laugh? I blame the parents for the way children behave nowadays."

"What's more, she's got her eye on an island in the Pacific, or the Caribbean or somewhere—haven't you, Jill? I daresay she'll invite you to stay, Katie."

"Oh Daddy!" cried Jill, giving him a very loving look. "You said you were sick of hearing about it."

"So I was. But you've kept quiet about it for at least

a fortnight. Well, we shall know one way or the other this coming Saturday, your mother tells me. Isn't that right?"

"Yes—it's on television."

"What do you think of that, Katie?" he asked her. "We'll soon be off to grow orchids in the South Seas!"

Aunt Katie laughed, but not as though she enjoyed doing so. "He's too absurd, Margaret," she said to her sister.

It was on Thursday morning that something rather startling happened. Jill as usual collected the mail, which was left in a box by the gate. There was always quite a lot, envelopes of all sizes with catalogs and advertisements for her father, inquiries addressed to Hyde's Nursery, and personal letters from friends or relations. Also Mrs. Remnant's letters came to this box, and since she was such a keen gardener, she received almost as many catalogs as John Hyde. Jill liked to sort out the mail into piles and if there was time she would run down to the trailer with Mrs. Remnant's letters before she had her breakfast. At one time they had tried to get Brandy to collect the mail, for he was good at carrying things, but they gave it up after he ate two or three packages.

Today there was a long envelope that was not addressed to John Hyde, or to Mrs. Hyde, or even to Hyde's Nursery. It was not addressed to Mrs. Remnant or to Aunt Katie either. It was addressed to Jill Hyde

and Lambert Jeffreys, and it had the word FULLOWAG printed in red across one corner.

Jill let all the rest of the mail fall to the floor. She seized the envelope and held it, staring at the address, at the name in the corner. Then she looked around her desperately. She saw her father in one of the greenhouses. She ran to him, waving the envelope, calling to him so wildly that he came to the door instantly, as though he feared she must have something terrible to tell him.

"Fullowag," she gasped.

"Fullowag," he repeated, rather flatly. "Oh. That. What about it?"

"Letter, Daddy. Look. What do you think it says?"

"What?" Now he sounded quite alarmed.

"I don't know yet. I haven't opened it. I can't. It's for Limpet, too. Can I go and find him? Can I? Now? Before breakfast?"

"I should think you'd better," her father said.

At that moment, however, Limpet himself appeared, with two envelopes that had been put into the Jeffreys' box by mistake.

"Limpet! They've written to us! Fullowag! There's a letter—a letter from Fullowag, Limpet!"

"Come inside, both of you," John Hyde said. Putting a hand on the shoulder of each of them, he pushed them into the house. "Now," he said. "Open it."

Margaret Hyde, with two plates of bacon and eggs, came in at that moment from the kitchen.

"Jill, you'll be late for school. . . . Hello, Limpet —you're early, aren't you? What's happening?"

"A letter, Mummy," Jill cried. "Fullowag. It's from Fullowag. Do you think it's to say we've won?"

"Good gracious—" she began. She looked at her husband, then back at Jill and Limpet. "We shan't know unless you open it, shall we?"

"You're the eldest," Limpet said politely. "You open it, Jilly."

Jill's fingers were sticky with excitement. She could hardly hold the envelope, let alone tear it open.

"Here." Her father had picked up a knife from the

breakfast table. He slit the envelope and handed it back. "Now do get a move on," he said.

Jill pulled out the letter. She unfolded it. It was very short indeed.

"On no account," she read aloud, "forget to tune in to our Fullowag program next Saturday at 6:30 P.M. We shall have an announcement of interest to *you*."

It was only Thursday morning. There was all that day to get through, and Friday and Saturday until the evening. . . . How would they live through the time?

"Now keep perfectly calm," John Hyde said. "Jill— Limpet . . . keep calm. Remember a great many people must have entered the contest. This is probably just a reminder—a sort of advertisement. You know what I mean, don't you? They want everybody to see their program. That's understandable. But it need not mean anything more than that. I don't think for a moment it does mean more than that. Do you, Margaret?"

"I—suppose not," she said. And Jill knew that her mother had been going to say *I hope not,* and had changed the words at the last minute.

"But if it's for everybody, Daddy—why does it have *you* underlined? It says an announcement of interest to *you*."

"I know it looks like business," he agreed. "But you see, Jill, when it comes to advertising almost anything can seem possible. Anyway, my dear, there's nothing we can do about it, is there? We'll just have to wait until Saturday. Now get on with your breakfast, as quick as you can."

Jill slid into her place at the table. The bacon was already cold, but however delicious it had been, she would not have been able to eat it. She cut it up and pushed it about. She would have liked to go away and lie down somewhere in the dark until Saturday evening came. She felt rather sick, not only with excitement, but with a kind of dread. Somewhere in the background she heard her parents talking together quietly—rather as though there were some trouble in the family which they found it necessary but difficult to discuss. "Tapsells," was one word she heard. And something about "I can't imagine what they'd say. . . ." But Jill was too busy with her own worries to try to work that one out.

She knew that both her parents were worried, and she knew why. They were afraid that she and Limpet really were going to win the island. They did not want this to happen. Worse still, she knew now that not even Limpet wanted it to happen. And worst, very worst of all—she was no longer certain that she wanted it to happen herself.

9

The Final Result

It was Saturday. It was six o'clock. So it was just half an hour from the start of the Fullowag program.

The television set had been tuned in for hours in case at the last minute they might not have been able to get it loud and clear. Since five o'clock Jill and Limpet had been arranging and rearranging the chairs for those who would come to watch. First they made a semicircle around the set, then they decided those at the end might not see very well, so they made two straight rows. Then they went back to a semicircle. There were only six people to arrange for, but it seemed a huge crowd. Besides Jill and Limpet there would be Jill's parents, Aunt Katie and Mrs. Remnant. And of course Brandy, who would not need a chair and might not even bother to watch the program.

"What about your mother and father, Limpet?"

"Dad's at a cricket game and Mum's watching another program."

"I do think they might be a bit interested. They must see how excited you are."

"I'm not excited. I'm frightened."

"Why did you ever go in for the contest, then, if you didn't want to win?"

"*You* wanted to win," said Limpet.

Jill did not answer that. By turns she herself was miserable and joyful, hot and cold, excited and terrified. She knew what Limpet meant.

Gradually the hands of the clock ticked around, and the programs before Fullowag played themselves away. At twenty past six Mrs. Remnant and Brandy came up from Little Paddock. At twenty-two minutes past, Jill's mother came and sat down next to Mrs. Remnant. Brandy roamed about the room. There was no sign of John Hyde, no sign of Aunt Katie.

"Why don't they come?" cried Jill.

The program was just beginning when they arrived. The Fullowag tune was playing, the Fullowag Fidos were singing, but Aunt Katie came in talking at the top of her voice.

"*Sssshhhh!*"

"What? What's the matter? Oh—has it started? Am I late? Where shall I sit?"

The noise seemed to go on and on. Even Brandy was settled by now and it seemed to Jill and Limpet that he was watching the screen as eagerly as they were—probably because the word *biscuit* was being used so much. Aunt Katie's voice disturbed him. He got up and began to fidget about, almost as though a walk would be a good idea. Mrs. Remnant called to him, and although her voice was soft it added to the general dis-

turbance until it was impossible to know what was going on on the screen.

Then at last there was quiet as the music changed to the sound of guitars and soft singing. Palm trees filled the picture, water broke on long reefs; the sun shone on white sands, on trees and bushes covered with flowers, on canoes riding the surf that stretched for miles. . . .

Then came a man wearing a wreath of flowers around his neck. He was the Fullowag man. He explained about the contest, about the island, the sun, the sea, the charming custom of greeting newcomers with garlands like the one he was wearing. "You, too," he told them, "can enjoy these things—and through Fullowag. Which of you lucky people is our prizewinner? Which of you is now the proud owner of an island in those southern seas? . . ."

Jill sat with her hands clenched between her knees. Limpet was standing up by now, looking as though he would willingly step right into the box and hurry the man along with what he was saying.

"I can't see a thing, Limpet," Aunt Katie said, in a loud voice. "Do sit down, there's a good boy."

". . . introduce our winner to you all," the Fullowag man was saying when quiet returned. "Proud owner of an enchanted island! She is here in the studio with me. Give her a hand, everybody!"

Jill looked around quickly. For a second she felt she

was actually in the television studio and that everyone sitting at home was watching her. Then she saw that both her parents had suddenly relaxed and smiled at one another. That meant—well, of course it meant that the silly-looking woman now bowing and grinning on the screen was the winner of the contest—it meant that after all Jill and Limpet had failed in their attempt. . . .

"It isn't us!" Jill cried. "It isn't us!"

Her father put his arm around her and pulled her against his knee. "All for the best," he said. "Don't you think so? It's all right here, isn't it? I don't think we've got such a bad old home that we need to leave it."

Suddenly all the days and weeks of thinking that she and Limpet would certainly, would almost certainly be the winners crowded over Jill like the surf breaking on those faraway reefs. That first wave was followed by another, and then another—of relief and warmth, of gladness that the whole silly business was over, and of wonder that she had ever felt it to be so important. She would never be able to explain why she had been so stubborn about Fullowag. . . .

"You're missing the program," her mother said.

"I don't care anymore. It's won. It's all over. Can't you switch it off?"

The screen was still full of the Fullowag man, the Fullowag Fidos were singing the winning slogan set to a jingly little tune—*Fullowag, Fullowag, pounds of pleasure in each bag.* . . . Then they faded out and the Fullowag man began reading names from a list.

"It's the hundred consolation prizes," Limpet said.

All sorts of people they had never heard of and would never meet had won electric toasters, tape recorders, folding dinghies, deck chairs, camping outfits, beach umbrellas, tents, hair dryers. . . .

"Listen to that!" cried Mrs. Remnant, who was by now the only one of them still watching with any attention.

"I will repeat those names," said the Fullowag man, exactly as if he had heard her. "A consolation prize of a camping outfit to Jill Hyde and Lambert Jeffreys. Jill and Lambert are our youngest competitors. Are you there, Jill? Are you watching, Lambert?"

"Yes! Yes!" shouted Lambert.

"Remember—I said there'd be something of special interest to *you*. Congratulations, Jill and Lambert. And happy camping!"

"Send it soon!" Limpet urged him, jigging with excitement.

"It's in the mail for you," said the obliging Fullowag man as, still smiling, he faded from the picture.

"It'll be here on Monday, then," said Limpet. "A camping set, Jilly. That'll be a tent and things. Better than an island all those miles away. More useful."

"Is it true? Are you sure he means it?" Jill said.

"Of course he means it," said Aunt Katie, much surprised. "Fancy hearing my clever niece's name coming out of the set like that! Who would have thought it?"

The telephone bell was ringing out in the hall as they all chattered together in their excitement. John Hyde went to answer it.

"It was Mr. Tapsell," he said when he returned. "He and Miss Tapsell are home from their vacation. He says the roses have got covered with greenfly while he's been away. I said I'd let him have some of my special spray. Jill—run around with it for me, will you?"

"*Now*, Daddy?"

"Yes—now. Limpet will go with you. And I daresay Mrs. Remnant would be glad of a run for Brandy."

"But we want to talk about the camping outfit."

"You can talk as you go," he replied firmly.

After all the Fullowag excitement, being sent on an errand seemed a terrible letdown.

When they reached Windle Lodge, they found to their surprise that Mr. Tapsell and his sister were out by the front door watching for them.

"We saw the television program," Miss Tapsell cried, just as though nothing unusual had happened, just as though they had never been away. "We felt proud to know such a clever pair."

"And it's no good pretending," her brother said. "We are very happy indeed that you did *not* win the island in the South Seas."

"We were afraid we might lose you just as we'd got

to know you," Miss Tapsell explained. Then she
seemed to see that Jill and Limpet were looking quite
bewildered, and she blushed and said, "There may
have been a little misunderstanding."

"The new fence, Miss Tapsell. . . ."

"All the notices. . . ."

"The notices were never ordered—that was a mistake. But the fence seems necessary. Now—please come
with us. We have something to show you."

Miss Tapsell led the way out of the house. As she
crossed the garden with the rest behind her, she was
making anxious little noises, almost like a bird twitter-
ing—as though something were about to happen that
had been planned with great care, and if the planning
went wrong, then she would simply not know how to
bear the disappointment.

By now the sun was gone, but the clear twilight of
summer lay over Windle Wood and the primrose sky
was mirrored in the quiet lake. Miss Tapsell had led
them a little way along the side of the grass slope, so
that they were looking down slightly on the water.

But something had happened to it. Something was
changed. The pile of stones had gone, so the hole must
have been filled. But there was more than that. From
the shore to the island a little bridge had been built,
and the grass that led to it had been clipped into a
green inviting path. Miss Tapsell stood back. Then she
gave Jill a little push, and Limpet after her, so that
they both began to run down the path as it wound gen-

tly to the lake and the bridge. At the shore end of the bridge there was a gate.

Jill touched it rather timidly. "It's locked," she said.

"And here," said Mr. Tapsell, "is the key. Take it. Keep it—it's yours. It also unlocks a gate in the fence beyond the wood. So you can come and go as you please."

"And about the misunderstanding," said Miss Tapsell. "We found we could only keep our idea a secret by going away and locking you out of Windle. We explained to your parents, of course. But all this time we have been so afraid you might win the contest after all."

Jill and Limpet stood by the gate, not knowing what to say. Not knowing, really, what to think—for had they really heard what they thought they had heard?

"Do you mean we can go through the gate?" Limpet said at last.

"It's yours! It's yours!" cried Mr. Tapsell and Miss Tapsell. "Do as you wish!"

Limpet had the key, so he slid it into the lock and turned it, and sure enough the gate opened. He stepped inside, and Jill followed, and Brandy.

"Has the island got a name?" Jill asked.

"Most certainly. This," said Miss Tapsell, "is Surprise Island."

As she spoke she was moving away, and her brother with her.

"Excuse us," he murmured. "Getting along

now . . . things to do. . . . See you another time.
. . . Soon . . . Soon. . . ."

They were out of earshot before any thanks could be
spoken. And even now, Jill thought, and Limpet
thought too, it was difficult to know if it could be really
true. Surprise Island. . . . Theirs? Truly?

Now at last they stood on the island, where the thin
tree stood motionless in the still evening air.

"What's in the parcel?" Limpet asked, whispering.

At the last minute, Miss Tapsell had thrust a pack-
age into Jill's hands. Now she undid the wrapping.
There was something soft inside that unfolded itself.

It was a flag.

It was made of very thick silk, and on it Miss Tapsell
had embroidered a map of the island, and three initials
—J for Jill, L for Limpet, B for Brandy. . . .

"It's true! It's true!" Jill cried. "Limpet, it's true!"

She began dashing about the tiny island, holding the
flag so that it streamed out above her in the breeze she
made. Limpet ran after her, catching her excitement,
wild with happiness, shouting to Brandy, and calling as
he went—

"That's Hyde Harbor. . . . Here's Brandy Bay. . . ."

"And Limpet Lagoon. . . ."

"Lambert Lagoon," he corrected.

"Yes, all right."

"We need a flagpole, Jilly. My father can make one."

"All right," she said again.

After a long time of looking, of understanding at last that the wonderful thing had happened and they had an island of their own after all, they folded the flag carefully, locked the gate behind them and went slowly home.

"See you tomorrow," said Limpet.

"See you tomorrow. You bring the key. I'll bring the flag. We'll stay all day."

Brandy was always just as glad to get home as he was to set out, and already he was hurrying back to Little Paddock and Mrs. Remnant. There was something about his tail as he went that made Jill and Limpet burst out laughing.

"He's full of wags!" cried Jill.

And then they both shouted out together—"*And so are we!*"